WELCOME TO Pump Street Primary

Meet some of the children ...

Barry Barsby

Daisy Poborski

Rashid Ali

Floella Potts

Freddie Stanton

Monica Bellis

... in Miss Twigg's class

Craig Soapy

Karen Smart

Terry Flynn

Fatima Patel

Lily Wongsam

Paul Dimbley

Titles in the Pump Street Primary series

THIS IS BOB WILSON

He wrote this story
and drew the pictures.

He lives in the Derbyshire countryside in a
house which he designed and built himself
from an old cowshed. He has three grown-up
children and nine grandchildren. When he
was young he wanted to be a pop star, and
he started to write songs. He became an art
teacher and wrote plays and musicals, and
shows for television and radio. Then he began
to write and illustrate stories for children. He
is the author of the *Stanley Bagshaw* picture
books and the best-selling *Ging Gang Goolie,
It's an Alien!*

First published 2000 by Macmillan Children's Books
a division of Macmillan Publishers Limited
25 Eccleston Place, London SW1W 9NF
Basingstoke and Oxford
www.macmillan.com

Associated companies throughout the world

ISBN 0 330 37090 1

3 5 7 9 8 6 4 2

A CIP catalogue record for this book is available from
the British Library.

Printed and bound in Great Britain by Mackays of Chatham plc, Kent

Visit Bob Wilson's website at www.planetbob.co.uk

Barry's Bear

written and illustrated by
Bob Wilson

MACMILLAN CHILDREN'S BOOKS

Here are some of the school staff ...

Mr C Warrilow BSc MEd

Miss Twigg

Mr Manley

Mr Boggis

Mrs York

Mr Lamp-Williams

Miss Gaters

Mrs Jellie

Norman Loops

Janice

Mrs Brazil

For Ami, Thomas, Elias,
Matilda, Reuben, Alexander,
Marius, Lucien and Babik

THIS IS BARRY BARSBY

At least it *should* have been.

Barry Barsby is always late for everything.
Even his school photograph.
Miss Twigg, our class teacher, says he
is "the bane of her life".

Barry Barsby, where have
you been? You should have
been here at 2 o'clock.

Why?
What happened?

If other children are late for school they'll have a good excuse. For example, they'll say something like,

Or maybe . . .

But Barry Barsby has got what Miss Twigg calls "an overactive imagination". *(I think she means that he tells fibs.)* He'll say something like,

Sorry I'm late, Miss. My watch stopped and I thought it was still yesterday.

Or maybe . . .

Sorry I'm late, Miss. I got knocked off my bike by this ENORMOUS WASP!

Miss Twigg always says the same thing.
She waits until Barry has quite finished,
then she says, "Barry Barsby, I don't
think that's funny . . . *or* clever."
Then she turns to the rest of us
and says, "Don't laugh. You'll only
encourage him." And puts a very stern
look on her face.

Miss Twigg's
STERN face

Sometimes she keeps the stern look
on her face right through till the first
playtime.

*(I think when she gets into the
staffroom she relaxes a bit.)*

Once, when he was *really* late getting back to the bus after swimming,
                     Barry Barsby said,

Sorry I'm late, Miss. This HUGE OCTOPUS with hundreds of legs crawled up out of the shower plughole and tried to eat my underpants.

Karen Smart (who's very clever)* said,

Actually, Barry, it couldn't have been an octopus. An octopus has EIGHT legs.

And Miss Twigg burst out laughing. But the bus driver had been kept waiting.
He said it was *no laughing matter, he'd a good mind to complain to the head teacher.*

* At least she thinks she is.

Then Miss Twigg stopped laughing.
And she said that it *wasn't funny*.
She said that it *was not funny at all*.
She said that one day Barry Barsby's
overactive imagination would get him
into *big trouble*.
And it did.
Last Thursday, when we went on a trip
to Crampton Ponds and Nature Park,
Barry Barsby's overactive imagination
got him into . . .

Really Really

BIG
TROUBLE

(The sort of trouble that's brown and
hairy and . . . *wears a bowler hat!*)

"Now listen carefully," said Miss Twigg. "On Thursday we are going to go to Crampton Ponds and Nature Park. It's a special sort of park reserved for wildlife."

Here you will be able to see all sorts of wild animals in their natural surroundings.

CRAMPTON PONDS
ATURE PAR

You mean like polar bears and penguins?

said Paul Dimbley.

Miss Twigg said, "No, Paul. Not polar bears and penguins."

Karen Smart (who's very clever) said, "You don't get polar bears in England. Do you, Miss?"

After everybody* had come back into the classroom after first playtime, Miss Twigg handed out a list.

It was a list of things that we'd got to take on the trip.

Pump Street Primary School
Head teacher: Mr C. Warrilow

Pump Street
Burston-on-Tweddle
Derbyshire
DE6 2GP

Tel: (01335) 324632

Re: TRIP TO CRAMPTON PONDS
AND NATURE PARK
Thursday 8th June

You will need to bring:

From school

(1) Your best drawing book.
(2) Pencils or crayons (*not* felt tips) and a rubber.
(3) Nature notebook (the one you've been using for this term's topic).

From home

(1) Picnic lunch, preferably in plastic lunch box.
(2) Cagoule and a waterproof hat. (I know it's June but it still might rain.)
(3) Sensible footwear. *Old* trainers (*not* your best shoes).

<u>PLEASE NOTE</u>

The bus will leave from outside the school at EIGHT O'CLOCK

Everybody was reading their list when
Barry Barsby arrived.

> Sorry I'm late, Miss.
> The cloakroom was full of
> polar bears and I couldn't find
> space to hang my coat up.

Miss Twigg didn't say the usual thing
about Barry not being funny or clever.
She just smiled, handed him his list
and said,

> Barry, this list is for you.
> I want you to note the bit
> that I have UNDERLINED
> at the bottom.

Barry's list:

Pump Street Primary School
Head teacher: Mr C. Warrilow

Pump Street
Burston-on-Tweddle
Derbyshire
DE6 2GP

Tel: (01335) 324632

Re: TRIP TO CRAMPTON PONDS AND NATURE PARK
Thursday 8th June

You will need to bring:

From school

(1) Your best drawing book.
(2) Pencils or crayons (*not* felt tips) and a rubber.
(3) Nature notebook (the one you've been using for this term's topic).

From home

(1) Picnic lunch, preferably in plastic lunch box.
(2) Cagoule and a waterproof hat. (I know it's June but it still might rain.)
(3) Sensible footwear. *Old* trainers (*not* your best shoes).

PLEASE NOTE

The bus will leave from outside the school at **SEVEN** O'CLOCK.

IT WAS THE DAY OF THE TRIP

It was Barry Barsby.

"That's all right, Barry," said Miss Twigg. "I quite understand. Just get on the bus."

Where is everybody?

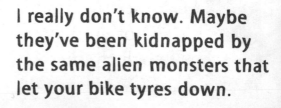

I really don't know. Maybe they've been kidnapped by the same alien monsters that let your bike tyres down.

By 8 o'clock everybody had arrived.
Miss Twigg said,

The bus driver said, "Right you are."
He folded up his newspaper and put it
under his seat. Which was unfortunate
because that meant that Miss Twigg
didn't get to see the headline on the
front page. Not until afterwards
anyway. By which time . . .
IT WAS MUCH TOO LATE!

CIRCUS ANIMALS ESCAPE SHOCK!

Six penguins, an ostrich and a **large brown bear** are reported to have escaped from **Blount Brothers' Circus.** They are thought to be somewhere in the region of **Crampton Ponds and Nature Park.** POLICE WARN PUBLIC. Police have issued a warning to the public to stay indoors and if they do

**MR OSCAR BLOUNT,
CIRCUS OWNER**

see the beasts, *not to go anywhere near them,* **especially the bear.**

"You'll be able to recognise the bear," said Chief Inspector Willaby Cloone. "It will be *wearing a bowler hat.*"

A BOWLER HAT, SIMILAR TO THE ONE WORN BY THE BEAR

Crampton Ponds. A peaceful scene. But for how long?

MAD BEASTS
are not in the least bit
DANGEROUS!
(claims circus expert)

"These are certainly not wild animals," a circus spokesman told our reporter. "They are not in the least bit dangerous. Not at all. Well, not *really* dangerous. At least, the penguins are OK and the ostrich only kicks people now and again. And the huge brown bear is very friendly really. Well . . . err . . . most of the time. **As long as he's not hungry."**

WHAT DO BEARS EAT?

The public need to know.
"Is it a man-eating bear, for instance?" asked Mr Lucien Wimp. "Or could it be," said his wife Jill, "that it's a woman-eating bear?"

For some reason the bus driver didn't seem all that keen to go to Crampton Ponds and Nature Park.

But we got there eventually.

CRAMPTON
The Home of
ENGLISH
NATURE

When we were all off the bus Miss Twigg said, "Gather round." And she explained what our first task was to be.

I want you to spread out along the edges of the pond — and keep your eyes peeled. If you see anything interesting or unusual, I want you to draw it.

We were to meet up with Miss Twigg in the open space by the boat yard at 11 o'clock – *and not be late*.

Miss Twigg said that there was some interesting and unusual wildlife to be seen around the edge of the pond.

And she was right.

Barry Barsby saw something
really unusual.

At 11 o'clock everybody* met up with Miss Twigg in the open space by the boat yard. She was very interested to know what we had seen and drawn.

Line up in alphabetical order and I'll come to you one at a time.

*Well, not quite everybody.

Julie Abberton was first.

Julie Abberton had seen millions and millions and millions of tadpoles.

And a green frog with yellow stripes down its back and little brown spots on its legs. It was REALLY BEAUTIFUL, Miss.

"Well, I never," said Miss Twigg.

I hope you've drawn me a REALLY BEAUTIFUL picture.

Julie gave her picture to Miss Twigg.

Julie's picture.

"It's . . . er . . . very nice, Julie," said
Miss Twigg.

"Couldn't draw the frog," said Julie.

It kept moving.

Rashid Ali was next. Rashid had seen an unusual snail crawling across a big stone.

It had got a black-and-white striped shell and great big horns sticking out of its head. It was REALLY FANTASTIC, Miss.

"I hope you've drawn me a *really fantastic* picture," said Miss Twigg.

Rashid's picture.

"It's . . . er . . . very good, Rashid,"
said Miss Twigg.

"Couldn't draw the snail," said Rashid.

It was Barry Barsby's turn next.
At least, it *should* have been.

Miss Twigg said, "I might have known it.
That boy is the bane of my life."

And Paul Dimbley had to go next instead.

Paul Dimbley had seen an *incredibly beautiful* and *wonderfully fantastic* red, yellow and purple butterfly sitting on a leaf.

Would you like to see my picture, Miss?

But Paul Dimbley never got the chance to show Miss Twigg his drawing of a leaf because . . .

Miss, Miss! Sorry I'm late, Miss. Only you'll never guess what! I was down by the edge of the pond, just the other side of those tall weeds and—

But Miss Twigg didn't give Barry time to
make one of his silly excuses. She said,

So he did.

Barry's picture.

"Penguins!?" said Miss Twigg.

Why on earth have you drawn PENGUINS?

"Couldn't draw the ostrich," said Barry.

It kept moving.

Miss Twigg said,

Barry, I'll have a word with you about this. Later.

She carefully folded Barry's picture and put it in her pocket.
Then she gave us our next task. We were to explore the woods.
This time if we saw anything interesting we had to write down in our notebooks what we thought it might be.

Meet up with me in the picnic area at one-thirty. And DON'T be late.

As if.

Miss Twigg said that there was some really interesting and unusual wildlife to be found in the woods.

And she was right.

At half-past one everybody* met up with Miss Twigg in the woodland picnic area.
She was very interested to hear what we had observed and written about.

Right now. Let me see. Who shall we have to go first?

*Well, almost everybody

Karen Smart was first.

Karen Smart had seen a stoat running along the top of a stone wall.

> At least I THINK it was a stoat. It was either a stoat or a weasel.

"Well done, Karen," said Miss Twigg. "It's true. A stoat *does* look like a weasel." And she showed us a picture in a book so that we could see the difference.

Craig Soapy was next. Craig had seen a crow sitting high up in a tree.

At least I THINK it was a crow.
It was either a crow or a rook.

"Very good, Craig," said Miss Twigg.
"It's true. Rooks and crows do look very much alike."
And she showed us another picture.

They both look like blackbirds to me.

MEANWHILE,
in the woods
Barry Barsby
had noted
some *really
interesting
wildlife*.

!?

Terry Flynn was next. Terry was just about to tell us what he'd seen, when . . .

Miss, Miss!
Sorry I'm late, Miss.
Only I've just seen a—

Barry Barsby, have you no manners?
Don't you know that it's rude to interrupt when other people are speaking?
I'll tell you when it's your turn.

And she did . . . .

. . . eventually.

But first she let Terry Flynn tell us how he'd seen a hare . . . *that was either a hare or a rabbit.*

"Please, Miss?"

"Not yet, Barry."

Then Lily Wongsam told us about a moth . . . *that could have been a butterfly.*

"Please, Miss?"

"Not yet, Barry."

Then Karl Snape told us how he'd been very nearly stung on the nose by a bee . . . *that was either a bee, a wasp or a hornet.*

"Please please, Miss!?"

"All right, Barry," said Miss Twigg. "I give in. Tell us what you saw."

Barry said,

I saw a huge, brown, hairy business man sitting under a tree. At least I THINK it was a huge, brown, hairy business man.

Miss Twigg said, "Barry Barsby! That is not the least bit funny *or* clever. I want a word with you . . ."

Then, thinking she heard sniggering, she turned to the rest of us.

But none of us *were* laughing. We weren't even *tempted* to laugh. And none of us started to get our lunch boxes out either. Our minds were on something else.

Something that was not
the least bit funny . . .
. . . *or* clever.

When at last Miss Twigg saw what we'd seen she didn't seem to think that it was funny or clever either.
Actually I'm not sure what she was thinking . . .

But what she
        said was . . .

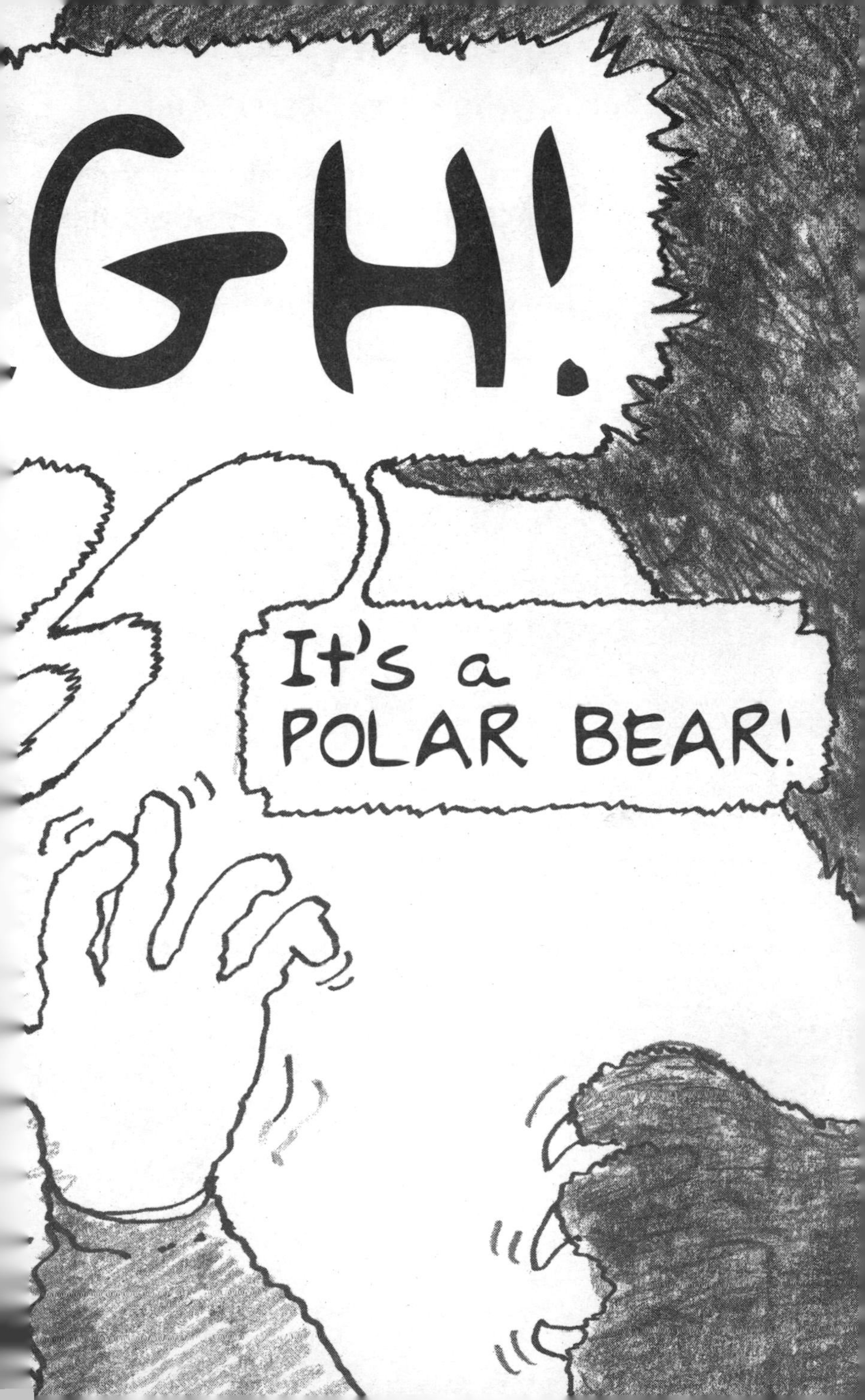
GH!
It's a POLAR BEAR!

Karen Smart (who's very clever)* said,

Paul Dimbley (who's quite good at noticing things) said,

Miss Twigg didn't really care what sort of bear it was. What she wanted to know was . . . *what to do about it.*

When she'd been training to be a teacher she'd been given a very useful book.

It was called . . .

A GUIDE FOR TRAINEE TEACHERS
(your questions answered)

Part 3: Dealing with awkward situations

Q What should a teacher do if a boy says something really really stupid in class and everybody else starts to giggle?

A The teacher should say, "I don't think that is funny or clever," then put on a very stern face and warn the rest of the class not to laugh.

Q What should a teacher do if there is an important visitor in class and someone in the front row lets off a smelly trump?

A The teacher should say, "I think it's a bit stuffy in here," and open a window. Then (making sure that the important visitor can't see) give the boy or girl thought to be responsible *a very piercing look*.

Q What should a teacher do if he or she is out of school on a nature trip and the class is attacked by a large brown bear?

A The teacher should shout **AARGH!** very loudly *and then start to worry.* (NB If the bear looks hungry the teacher should start to get *really worried*.)

Miss Twigg looked at the bear.
She started to get *really* worried.
Paul Dimbley said,

Karen Smart explained that brown
bears usually ate bananas, bamboo nuts
and sugar-frosted cornflakes.
"It's only the Black Belgian Maniac
Bear that eats schoolchildren, isn't it,
Miss?"
To which Miss Twigg replied,

It was just then that Craig Soapy said something really useful. He said,

I once saw a film on the telly about a circus and there was this brown bear that wore a bowler hat and its trainer said that the thing it liked to eat most of all were cucumber sandwiches.

Please, Miss. I've got cucumber sandwiches,

said Lily Wongsam.

Barry Barsby said,

I'll give him one then, shall I?

But Miss Twigg said, "NO! Don't you
go near that bear. *Barry, do you hear
what I say?* (You're not being funny or
clever.)
Barry. Don't you dare give that
bear a sandwich!

Barry, come back.

You'll be
EATEN
ALIVE!"

But he wasn't.
The bear simply took the sandwich
from Barry, looked at it . . . then said,

Afterwards, Karen Smart said that this
was probably brown bear talk for
"Thank you very much. Mmmmm . . .
cucumber, my favourite".
And Miss Twigg said that she was
probably right. But at the time, Miss
Twigg didn't say very much at all.

PUMP STREET PRIMARY
titles available from Macmillan

1. Dangerous Daisy   0 330 37092 8   £3.50
2. Barry's Bear   0 330 37090 1   £3.50
3. Flying Flo   0 330 37094 4   £3.50
4. Football Fred   0 330 37091 X   £3.50
5. Monica's Monster   0 330 37093 6   £3.50
6. Rashid's Rescue   0 330 37095 2   £3.50

All Macmillan titles can be ordered at your local bookshop
or are available by post from:

Book Service by Post
PO Box 29, Douglas, Isle of Man IM99 1BQ

Credit cards accepted. For details:
Telephone: 01624 675137
Fax: 01624 670923
E-mail: bookshop@enterprise.net

Free postage and packing in the UK.
Overseas customers: add £1 per book (paperback)
and £3 per book (hardback).

The prices shown below are correct at the time of going to press.
However, Macmillan Publishers reserve the right to show new retail
prices on covers which may differ from those previously advertised.

RASHID'S RESCUE

Miss Twigg says

If all my class were like Rashid my life would be free of stress.

But when she takes the children on a factory visit something happens to change her mind.

I nearly get glooped and grundled by a Galvanised Gasket Gargler!

MONICA'S MONSTER

Miss Twigg likes animals. But when Monica
brings little Samantha to school and says

Please, Miss,
would you like to see
my pet?

Miss Twigg says

NO!

FOOTBALL FRED

Fred's a dancer, not a goalie. When Miss
Twigg picks him for the match
against St Mildred's, he says

I'll do the best
I can, Miss.

But will Fred's best
be good enough?

YES!

FLYING FLO

Flo is the smallest girl in her class. But that doesn't stop her having big ideas. Miss Twigg says she'll go a long way.

And at the school fête she nearly does.

I think she's heading in the general direction of China.

DANGEROUS DAISY

Miss Twigg wants the head
teacher to get a surprise
on his birthday.
Thanks to Daisy . . .

He gets a REALLY
BIG surprise!

Daisy's not a naughty girl.
But she does tend to blow
things up.

THE END

Sorry I'm late, sir, only the playground's been taken over by a troupe of performing elephants and I couldn't find anywhere to park my bike.

Mr Warrilow said,

Oh, my goodness me! I hope they're not sitting on top of my brand-new car!

And everybody laughed.
They thought that the head teacher was being really funny *and* clever.

At least he *should* have been.

Mr Warrilow, the head teacher, thanked
Mr Blount very much indeed. He said
he was very kind. Then he said,

I will now ask Barry Barsby to
step forward and accept the free
tickets on behalf of the school.

Barry Barsby was up on the stage with
the teachers.

Next morning in assembly we had an important visitor. It was Mr Oscar Blount, the co-owner of Blount's Circus. He said,

I am most grateful that you should find my bear. And to thank you I have here tickets for the whole school to come to my circus for free.

Oh, it was no problem.
No problem at all. We teachers are trained to deal with this sort of thing.

As he was leaving, the trainer turned to Miss Twigg and said, "Oh by the way. I don't suppose you've noticed six penguins and an ostrich knocking about anywhere, have you?" Miss Twigg looked at Barry. Barry looked at Miss Twigg. And she smiled.

Don't laugh. It will only encourage me,

said Barry Barsby.

By the time the animal trainer from the circus arrived, the large brown bear was full to bursting and fast asleep.

The trainer thanked us all for finding his bear and looking after it so well. Miss Twigg said,

Barry seemed to get on well with the
bear.

Certainly
would.

I think he'd like some
cheese and onion crisps,
if anybody's got any.

Mark Walkerden had got cheese and
onion crisps.
The bear ate them.
Freddie Stanton had got a stick of
pepperami sausage going spare.
The bear ate that too.
The bear also ate:
    6 Mars Bars
    1 strawberry yoghurt
    3 apples
    12 slices of anchovy pizza
    1 jar of mustard
    and Paul Dimbley's plastic lunch box.